P9-CQV-285

WITHDRAWN

Dear Parent:

Congratulations! Your child is taking the first steps on an exciting journey. The destination? Independent reading!

STEP INTO READING® will help your child get there. The program offers five steps to reading success. Each step includes fun stories and colorful art. There are also Step into Reading Sticker Books, Step into Reading Math Readers, Step into Reading Phonics Readers, Step into Reading Write-In Readers, and Step into Reading Phonics Boxed Sets—a complete literacy program with something to interest every child.

Learning to Read, Step by Step!

Ready to Read Preschool–Kindergarten
• big type and easy words • rhyme and rhythm • picture clues
For children who know the alphabet and are eager to begin reading.

Reading with Help Preschool–Grade 1
• basic vocabulary • short sentences • simple stories
For children who recognize familiar words and sound out new words with help.

Reading on Your Own Grades 1–3
• engaging characters • easy-to-follow plots • popular topics
For children who are ready to read on their own.

Reading Paragraphs Grades 2–3
• challenging vocabulary • short paragraphs • exciting stories
For newly independent readers who read simple sentences with confidence.

Ready for Chapters Grades 2–4
• chapters • longer paragraphs • full-color art
For children who want to take the plunge into chapter books but still like colorful pictures.

STEP INTO READING® is designed to give every child a successful reading experience. The grade levels are only guides. Children can progress through the steps at their own speed, developing confidence in their reading, no matter what their grade.

Remember, a lifetime love of reading starts with a single step!

For my pumpkins,
Ramona and Leo
—A.J.

Copyright © 2010 Disney Enterprises, Inc. All rights reserved. The movie THE PRINCESS AND THE FROG Copyright © 2009 Disney, story inspired in part by the book THE FROG PRINCESS by E.D. Baker Copyright © 2002, published by Bloomsbury Publishing, Inc. Published in the United States by Random House Children's Books, a division of Random House, Inc., 1745 Broadway, New York, NY 10019, and in Canada by Random House of Canada Limited, Toronto, in conjunction with Disney Enterprises, Inc.

Step into Reading, Random House, and the Random House colophon are registered trademarks of Random House, Inc.

Visit us on the Web!
www.stepintoreading.com
www.randomhouse.com/kids

Educators and librarians, for a variety of teaching tools, visit us at
www.randomhouse.com/teachers

Library of Congress Cataloging-in-Publication Data
Jordan, Apple.
A fairy-tale fall / by Apple Jordan ; illustrated by Francesco Legramandi.
p. cm. — (Step into reading. Step 2)
"Disney princess."
Summary: Six Disney princesses enjoy Halloween activities in separate, easy-to-read vignettes.
ISBN 978-0-7364-2674-9 (trade) — ISBN 978-0-7364-8082-6 (lib. bdg.)
[1. Princesses—Fiction. 2. Halloween—Fiction. 3. Autumn—Fiction.] I. Legramandi, Francesco, ill. II. Title.
PZ7.J755Fb 2010 [E]—dc22 2009025964

Printed in the United States of America   10 9 8 7 6 5 4 3 2 1

STEP INTO READING®

STEP 2

Disney PRINCESS

A Fairy-Tale Fall

By Apple Jordan

Illustrated by Francesco Legramandi

CHILDREN'S LIBRARY

Random House 🏠 New York

WALLINGFORD PUBLIC LIBRARY
200 North Main St.
Wallingford, CT 06492

Halloween is here!
Snow White's
friends dress up.

Happy is a prince.

Grumpy is a bear.

Sleepy is a ghost.

Boo! Roar! Howl!

A princess's
haunted house is full
of fun!

Belle and the Beast
pick pumpkins.

There are so many
perfect pumpkins!
They look for
the best ones.

Belle brings
her pumpkins home.
She roasts the seeds.
She bakes a pumpkin pie.

Then she carves
the biggest pumpkin.

Sleeping Beauty goes
for a walk.

Her forest friends
join her.

Bright leaves fall
from the trees.

Sleeping Beauty brings a picnic to share.

14

Pumpkin muffins
and cider are
tasty treats!

Jasmine wants
a new costume.
She wants one
that is perfect
for a princess!

Aladdin brings her
a dream dress!

Jasmine and Aladdin
take a ride
on the Magic Carpet.

They give treats
to all their friends!

Ariel and her friends
have a costume party.

Everyone wears
a fancy mask.
No one knows
who is who!

Ariel and Flounder
ride the tail
of a whale.

Sebastian swims
into a seaweed forest.
Halloween is fun
under the sea!

Tiana leads
a Halloween parade.
She rides
on a spooky float.

Everyone cheers

for the royal parade.

The music is loud.
Ghosts and goblins
move to the beat!

Tonight is
the royal ball.

Cinderella makes
costumes for
all her friends.
Jaq is excited!

The Fairy Godmother
makes sure the
pumpkin carriage
is ready.

Bibbidi-bobbidi-boo!

Fall is the perfect time
for a pumpkin ride!

Marker noted 10/2010